The Parrots Go Bananas!

BRAVE BOOKS

Freedom Island

DOM-A-TRON

Doomsdome

THE OLD ISL

Burrycan

UTOPIA

WIGGAMORE WOOD

?

Rushington

SUMA SAVANNA

Hive Have

Furenzy Park

Toke-A-Toke

Wonder Well

Capitol

Mushroom Village

Deserted Desert

RAKA RAIN FOREST

Mt. Avalerif

Sky Tree

Snapfast Meadow

CAR-A-LAGO COAST

Starlotte City

Gray Landing

Home of the Brave

Welcome to Freedom Island, Home of the Brave, where good battles evil and truth prevails. Join Asher and Bongo as they navigate the challenges of fake news. Complete the BRAVE Challenge at the end of the book to learn more!

Watch this video for an introduction to the story and BRAVE Universe!

Saga Three: Tubular

Book 1

The Parrots Go Bananas!

Saga Three: Tubular—Book 1

The Parrots Go Bananas!

Book Illustrations © 2022 by Martín Morón
Map Illustration © 2021 by Ali Elzeiny

Published by BRAVE BOOKS
www.BRAVEbooks.com

ISBN: 978-1-955550-35-2 (paperback)

First edition published in the USA in 2023 by BRAVE BOOKS

Printed in Canada

The Parrots Go Bananas!

Sean Spicer and BRAVE BOOKS

Art by Martín Morón

BRAVE BOOKS

The biggest Smack-A-Ball game of the year was almost here, and Mushroom Village buzzed with excitement.

Fans sent pictures and notes back and forth through a new network of tubes they called Tubular.

A popular peacock named Penelope P sent more pictures through Tubular than anyone else. Penelope P had many thoughts, and wanted everyone to hear them. Only, the thoughts she sent out into the world weren't always totally true.

On the day of the big game, parrots flew down to Penelope P's picture-perfect rental mushroom. "Breaking news!" they squawked. "Bongo the Gorilla and Asher the Fox are coming to town for the Smack-A-Ball game!"

Penelope rolled her eyes, "Ugh, everyone loves Bongo and Asher, but I can't stand them. Like, they're so annoying and so good at everything. They're probably cheaters or something."

Sure enough, Bongo and Asher walked into Mushroom Village that very afternoon.

"Hey, Banana—I mean, Bonnie!" laughed Bongo.

"What are you wearing?"

Bonnie smiled, "I'm the mascot for our Smack-A-Ball team. Are you free this afternoon? The animals around here are so thankful for the way you saved Sky Tree. I know they'd love to have you play with us!"

Asher perked up. "That'd be epic!"

"Goooooooood evening, folks! It's a beautiful day in Mushroom Village, and it's looking like it's gonna be a faaaantastic game of Smack-A-Ball."

"Look! Team Apples and Team Bananas are shaking paws, and the ump's checked all their coco-ball smackers. Remember, players can use anything the umpire approves to hit those coco-balls."

"And we're off! What a game; the fans are sitting on the edge of their mushrooms."

"The Apples take the lead, 3-2."

"But wait! What a hit! That'll set the Bananas ahead by three."

As Bonnie cheered for her team, she noticed a group of parrots huddled in the shadows nearby snapping pictures of Asher and Bongo.

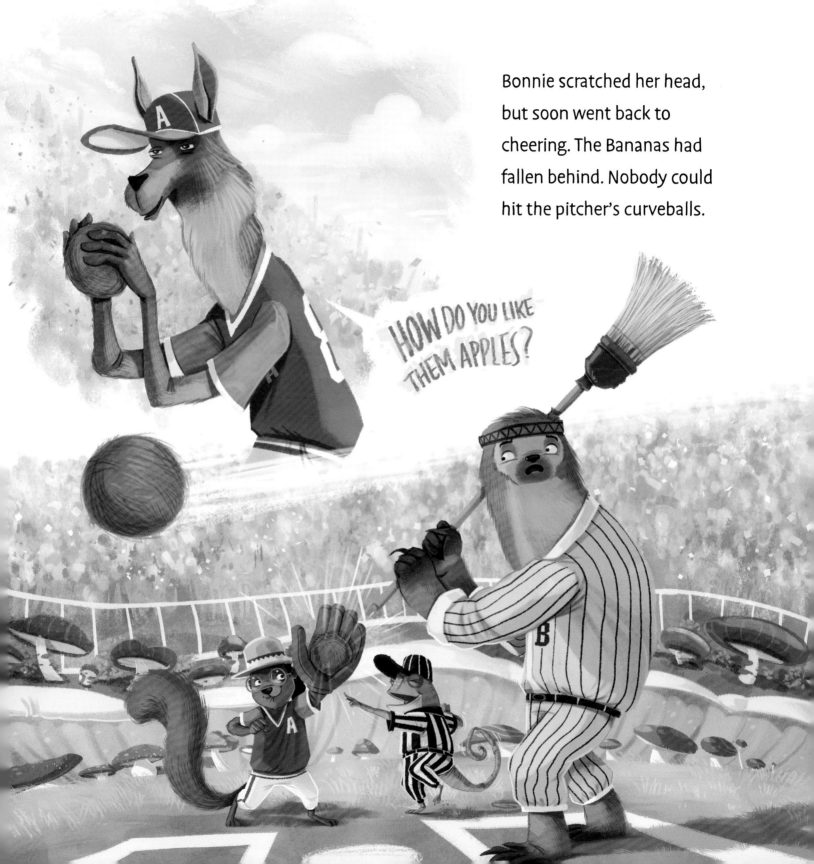

Bonnie scratched her head, but soon went back to cheering. The Bananas had fallen behind. Nobody could hit the pitcher's curveballs.

"We're down to the very last pitch, and things are not looking good for the Bananas. Bongo is their last hope. He'll need to smack this coco-ball out of the field to win the game."

"The crowd is holding its breath .... Here's the pitch ...."

The llama spit, stretched out his arm, and sent the coco-ball flying.

"HE'S DONE IT! The Bananas have won the game, and the crowd's going wild!"

That night, both teams threw one huge party to celebrate. They brought candy and cider and all sorts of fun things. And of course, they took a lot of pictures for Tubular.

But while the others celebrated, the parrots snapped picture after picture. "Penelope P will want to see this," they squawked, and sent another picture through the tube.

The next morning, as Bongo and Asher walked through the village, several animals sent them glares and stares.

One dog, who had looked so nice yesterday, gave them a nasty growl.

"Yo dog, what's up?" Bongo asked.

The dog barked. "Don't act like you don't know.
We're mad at you and that fox!"

Asher blinked. "Woah, woah. Are you upset because our team won the game?"

Penelope P strutted up. "Isn't it obvious? They're all angry because you cheated! I sent the photos all through Tubular, and now like the whole island knows. Just listen to the parrots."

"Team Bananas or Team Baloney?" a parrot announced. "Star player caught cheating in last night's game!"

"Bongo used his coconut cannon to shoot, not smack, a coco-ball, making him a cheater."

Penelope P slammed a picture into Asher's chest. "On top of cheating, Asher made fun of the other team by chomping into an apple right after he beat Team Apples."

"Yeah!" The crowd pressed forward. "You're cheaters, and you shouldn't stay in Mushroom Village."

"You shouldn't make fun of animals, that's not nice."

"Bongo and Asher are full of hate!"

"Get rid of the hate!"

Now all of Mushroom Village thought Bongo and Asher were no-good cheaters.

The crowd moved in, pressing Bongo and Asher toward the cliff. It seemed like they had nowhere to go when …

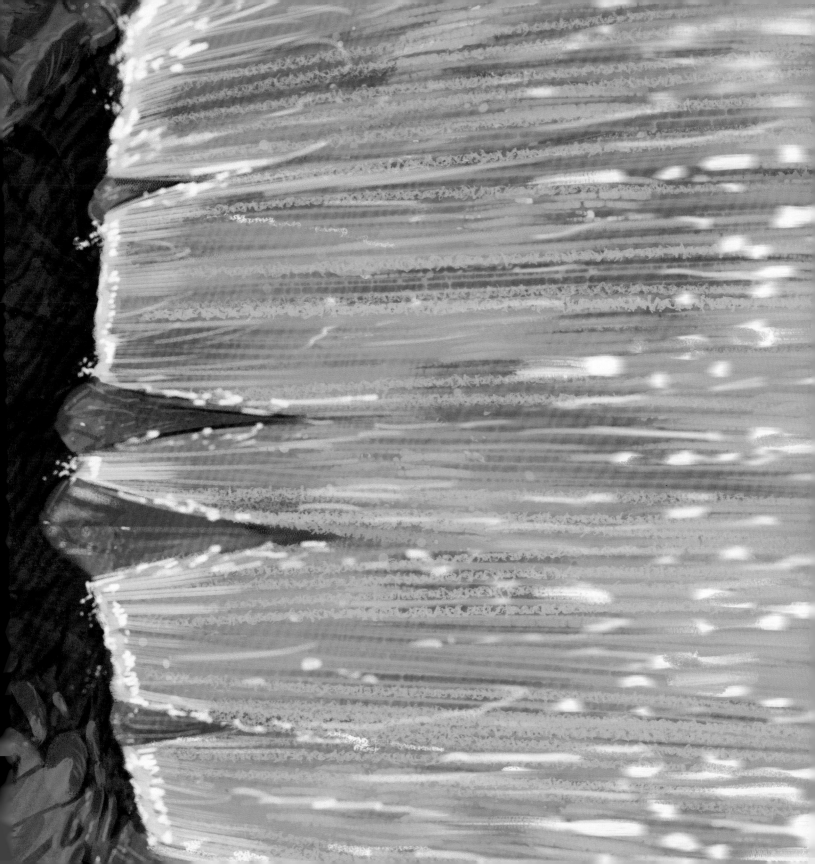

Bonnie the Bunny jumped up from the back of the crowd. "Please stop and think for a minute. Bongo and Asher are heroes of Freedom Island. Are they known for cheating? Why did you suddenly start believing they would do something awful?"

The animals paused and thought for a moment.

A sloth said, "Wait a second, the photos on Tubular came from Penelope P, and she's never liked Bongo and Asher."

The dog added on, "She wasn't even at the game yesterday!"

Bonnie held out her pictures. "I was at the game and took these. This picture proves Bongo was *hitting* the coco-ball, not shooting it." She held up another. "See this? This one shows the teams shaking paws after the ump approved all the smackers."

"And lastly, Asher wasn't making fun of the other team. *Everyone* was eating candy apples!"

The crowd had jumped to so many conclusions and accused Asher and Bongo before knowing all the facts. They sheepishly apologized for getting upset so quickly. Asher and Bongo forgave them, gratefully stepping away from the cliff.

But Penelope P did not apologize and fluttered away with the parrots behind her.

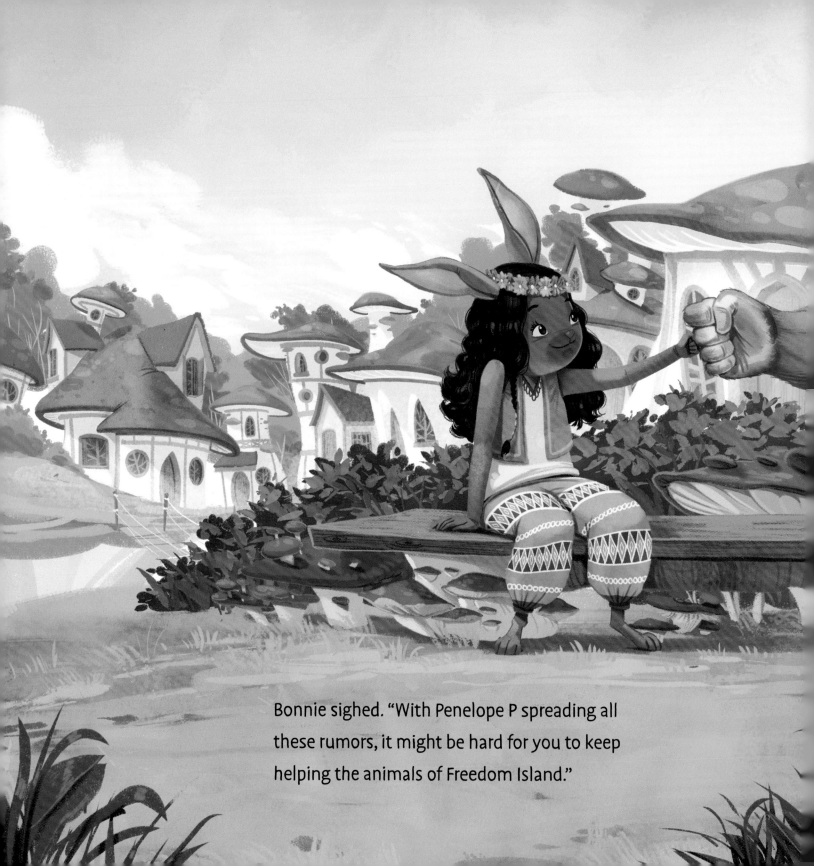

Bonnie sighed. "With Penelope P spreading all
these rumors, it might be hard for you to keep
helping the animals of Freedom Island."

Asher smiled, "Doing the right thing has never been easy. Anyways, we're glad to have friends like you, who don't listen to rumors."

The Fl!p Side

News of Mushroom Village

Issue 1

SMACK-A-BALL GAME OF THE YEAR WON BY THE BANANAS

Pirate Ship Debris Still being Found

Even after the reconstruction and cleanup completed in Sky Tree's canopy, citizens have discovered different trinkets and oddities around the town. One such citizen even found an in-tact pirate flag. "It's honestly perfect timing! I have been meaning to get a new blanket," stated Mrs. Squirrel.

THE DAILY WORD SCRAMBLE

How's it going my flip side readers? Today we have our special list of scrambled text that we need your help to make right!

EGVLIAL   NCUOCTO
NABNAA   PLAEP
CTIPUESR   SYNHETO

We hope you thought these weren't too "over-easy." And as always, stay on the sunny-side.

BRAVE CADETS,

Thankfully, Bonnie proved Asher and Bongo's innocence. But Penelope P. and her parrots are still spreading lies about Team BRAVE! Complete the three missions below to save the day:

- Update your map with the parrot and flag stickers included.

- Help Bongo and Asher in the BRAVE Challenge, and celebrate your victory with an epic reward.

- Can you find all 10 Tubular Tubes in the story?

Bongo and Asher are counting on you! Are you ready to be BRAVE?

Old Club Treehouse just Discovered

Remnants of what appears to be an old treehouse were found in the forest of Suma Savanna. Researchers believe this to be a gathering area for younger animals several years ago, as deduced from the words "Club Awesome Sauce" painted on the old, broken door.

Penelope P. flees Mushroom Village

Eye witnesses report spotting the pink and green influencer fluttering out of Mushroom Village. No word was given on her false accusation over the recent Smack-a-Ball game.

INTRODUCING...
SEAN SPICER

Sean Spicer is the host of Spicer & Co. on Newsmax. He served in the White House senior staff as Press Secretary and acting Communications Director for President Donald Trump. He received a master's degree from the Naval War College and serves in the U.S. Navy Reserve as Commander. Sean and his wife, Rebecca, have two children and live in Virginia. Sean is now joining with BRAVE Books in writing the book, *The Parrots Go Bananas!*, a story on fake news and will be popping up in the workbook to give advice about the topic. Learn more about him at SeanSpicer.com.

SEAN SUGGESTS:

"Hello families! I hope you will enjoy this BRAVE Challenge that helps your children understand the danger of false information and fake news."

INTRODUCTION

Team BRAVE is in trouble in Mushroom Village! Your mission for this BRAVE Challenge is to help the animals of Mushroom Village see the truth behind the fake information. To get started, grab a sheet of paper and a pencil, and draw a scoreboard like the one shown.

In the end, if your team can put more points on this scoreboard than the parrots, you have won the challenge and helped the animals learn the truth.

Before starting Game #1, choose a prize for winning. For example ...

BRAVE Cadets	Parrots
ⵊⵊⵊ I	II

- Baking cupcakes
- Having a family photoshoot
- Going to a baseball game or playing a family baseball game
- Whatever gets your kiddos excited!

GAME #1 - PICTURE PERFECT?

LESSON

When we're aware of how others can twist the truth, we're less likely to be deceived.

OBJECTIVE

The parrots have been spreading false information about Asher and Bongo with deceptive photos. BRAVE Cadets, help the animals of Mushroom Village learn the truth about what really happened!

MATERIALS

5 real photos and 5 fake or edited photos from the internet.

Optional photos for this game →

INSTRUCTIONS

1. Parents, use the suggested website or search the internet to find some "before and after" versions of edited photos. For example, you might find one photo of a dog in the backyard and an edited photo of the same dog set in outer space. Don't show the photos to the cadets yet!

2. Gather all the cadets together and show them the edited version of one photo. Do not tell them that it has been edited. Ask what they think of it.

3. Then show the other version of that same photo. Ask the cadets to guess which version is unedited.

4. Repeat this with all 4 other pairs of photos, sometimes showing the edited version first and sometimes the unedited. After each pair, have the cadets guess which is the original photo.

5. Make sure to tell the cadets which photo is the unedited photo after they have made their guess so they can see the difference.

SCORING

Every time the cadets guess correctly, award them 1 point.

For every incorrect guess, award the parrots 1 point.

TALK ABOUT IT

1. You had to spot the fake photos as a team during the game. Was it hard recognizing the photos that weren't real? Why or why not?

2. Did the edited photos look real before you saw the originals? What would happen if you always believed that everything you saw was true?

3. Sometimes, the media will twist the truth they're presenting to make the stories more exciting or to make their enemies look bad. What could happen if people believed everything on the news?

4. The animals of Mushroom Village blamed Asher and Bongo for cheating during the Smack-A-Ball game. What did the parrots do that made everyone believe that Bongo shot his coconut cannon to win the game? Why did changing the angle of the photo make Bongo look bad?

5. Has something you've heard or seen ever led you to believe something that wasn't true? How?

> "The righteous hates falsehood, but the wicked brings shame and disgrace."
>
> **Proverbs 13:5** (ESV)

6. How do people make a lie more believable? What should you do when someone shares false information?

SEAN SUGGESTS:

"People use many tactics to get you to believe lies. They can say it with other true things, or get important-sounding people to agree with them. We must be careful to check the things we see and hear, including things on the news."

GAME #2 - WHAT'S THAT SOUND?

LESSON

You must listen carefully so you can determine truths from lies.

OBJECTIVE

The animals of Mushroom Village believed what the parrots were saying about Asher and Bongo. BRAVE Cadets, help the animals realize that they shouldn't believe everything they hear!

MATERIALS

A blindfold for each cadet, and items listed within each round.

INSTRUCTIONS

1. Blindfold all of the cadets, and have them sit in the middle of the room.

2. **Secret Step:** *Parents, make sure you have access to the noise-making household items listed in the rounds below.*

3. A parent will make 2 noises in each round. The cadets should try to be quiet so they don't miss the sounds.

4. The cadets will have to guess what those 2 noises were when the round is finished. Once they guess the 2 noises and record the score, go on to the next round.

BRAVE TIP

Parents, feel free to create your own creative noises if you don't have access to one of the objects listed.

Round 1: Open a door; then close it.

Round 2: Knock on something wooden; then knock on something plastic.

Round 3: Open a bag of chips; then eat a chip.

Round 4: Drop a book; then flip a page in the book.

Round 5: Wave around a sheet of aluminum foil; then open an umbrella.

Round 6: Clap your hands; then stomp your feet.

Round 7: Take a sip of water; then pour out the water.

Round 8: Shake some keys; then wipe your feet on a mat or rug.

SCORING

Every time the cadets guess correctly, award them 1 point.

For every incorrect guess, award the parrots 1 point.

TALK ABOUT IT

1. In the game you had to guess the noises that were made. Was there a noise that you felt confident was correct but found out it was completely wrong?

2. What does it mean to jump to conclusions? Have you ever jumped to a conclusion about something because of what you heard? Why can that be dangerous?

3. The animals of Mushroom Village believed what the parrots and Penelope P said about Bongo and Asher. Why did the animals think that they cheated? What did the parrots and Penelope P say that made them believe this?

SEAN SUGGESTS:

"Fake news comes from people who don't have your best interests at heart. They want you to believe what is wrong without double checking. To check what someone is saying, we can look at other sources or ask people clarifying questions."

"Lying lips are an abomination to the Lord, but those who act faithfully are his delight."

Proverbs 12:22 (ESV)

4. Is there anyone on this earth that speaks honestly all the time? Why? Who always spoke the truth?

> "For to this you have been called, because Christ also suffered for you, leaving you an example, so that you might follow in his steps. He committed no sin, neither was deceit found in his mouth."
>
> **1 Peter 2:21-22** (ESV)

5. What can you do to check if someone is spreading wrong information? Who can you get advice from?

TALLY UP THE POINTS TO SEE IF YOU WON!

 ## FINAL THOUGHTS FROM SEAN

Fake news is when a person shares false information about someone or something. An example of this was when the parrots and Penelope P were telling animals that Bongo had cheated, when he clearly hadn't. Fake news is found in much of our world today whether it be on the television, social media, articles, or even what people are saying. When we encounter information on any platform, we need to be mindful of what we believe or think right away. To validate the source of information, we can check them against other news sources, ask people we trust, and look at Scripture to guide our thoughts and decisions.